# MiNA MiSTRY
## (sort of) INVESTIGATES

# BY ANGie LAKe

Sweet Cherry

Published by Sweet Cherry Publishing Limited
Unit 36, Vulcan House,
Vulcan Road,
Leicester, LE5 3EF
United Kingdom

First published in the US in 2020
2020 edition

2 4 6 8 10 9 7 5 3 1

ISBN: 978-1-78226-628-0

Mina Mistry (sort of) Investigates : The Case of the Loathsome School Lunches

Written by Angie Lake

Cover design by Ellie O'Shea and Amy Booth
Illustrations by Ellie O'Shea

www.sweetcherrypublishing.com

Printed and bound in India
I.TP002

# MINA MISTRY
## (sort of) INVESTIGATES

# THE CASE OF THE
# LOATHSOME SCHOOL LUNCHES

## ANGIE LAKE

# PERSONAL FILE:

**Name:** Mina Snotbridge a.k.a. Mina Mistry

**Occupation:** Student at Greenville Elementary

**Best Friend:** Mr. Panda

**Second Best Friend:** Holly Loafer

**Distinguishing Features:** Extreme intelligence and ambition. Destined to become a private investigator

**Hobbies:**

Playing the cello, investigating mysteries and spying on people

# LOG ENTRY #1

## Location: My bedroom
## Status: Bored

My name is Mina Mistry and this is my new secret log. **THIS IS NOT A DIARY.** I do have a diary, it's called *The Secret Diary of Mina Snotbridge*. That's my real name, not my secret undercover name. My secret undercover name is my mom's name from before she got married. I like **MiSTRY** because it sounds like mystery, and let's face it: **ANYTHiNG** is better than Snotbridge … Thanks Dad!

Anyway, my secret diary is pink and fluffy and girly. It has one of those useless locks that all diaries have, which all use the exact same key. It's badly hidden at the back of my sock drawer,

where absolutely anyone can find it. I try to write in it every day, but I don't write any details about the cases I'm investigating. I only write about the things that happen at school, what I've had for dinner and boring stuff like that.

I'm starting a new secret log today as my last one is already full. My secret log is where I write about my **iNVeSTiGATiONS**. I hide it under a conveniently loose floorboard at the **BACK OF MY CLOSeT**.

I also keep **personal files** on everybody I meet. I have a filing cabinet in my room where I **DON'T** keep these secret files, because … **DUH!**

I use the filing cabinet to keep my schoolwork and some old art projects made of dried pasta and glitter. The key is very poorly hidden at the front of my sock drawer.

I keep my secret personal files in my wardrobe. They're in a big box marked

**OLD TOYS** underneath some old toys.

I even keep a file on Mr. Panda.

# PERSONAL FILE:

**Name:** Mr. Panda

**Occupation:** Investigator

**Best Friend:** Mina Mistry

**Distinguishing Features:** Deep wisdom and an eye patch

**Hobbies:** Reading about extreme sports and practicing meditation

Mr. Panda is my **OLDEST** and **BEST** friend. I don't know how old Mr. Panda really is, I only know that my grandad got him for me when I was born and that he's been with me my **whole life**. He said that Mr. Panda would always look after me and he always has. He is always there to give me a cuddle when I'm feeling a bit down, to offer his **wisdom** and **Life experience** when I'm investigating cases, and to read to me from *Bungee Jumping Monthly* when I can't get to sleep.

Although Mr. Panda is my best friend, unfortunately he's **WAY** too old to go to school. My best friend at school is Holly Loafer.

# PERSONAL FILE:

**Name:** Holly Loafer

**Occupation:** Student at Greenville Elementary

**Best Friend:** Mina Snotbridge

**Distinguishing Features:** Blonde hair, strawberry lip gloss, cheerful personality (which can get a bit annoying), and a laser-like focus on her ambition of becoming a famous pop star

**Hobbies:** Dancing, collecting shoes and handbags (why?!), and chasing after Gareth Trumpshaw (DOUBLE WHY??!!)

Holly and I being best friends doesn't really make sense—we don't have much in common at all. Dad says we're more alike than we realize, but I don't see it!

Usually, school is quite samey, but today we had a bit of a change. **The school is hosting a series of talks on healthy eating.** This means they **CANCELLED** math so our class could go to the talk. Everyone seemed happy about missing math. I was just disappointed that we still had to do PE.

In our school no one likes PE because the class is run by the **TERRIFYING**

# HEALTHY EATING TALKS

## CLASSES CANCELLED

### SCHEDULE

CLASS A 10-11 A.M.

CLASS B 11 A.M. -12 P.M.

CLASS C 2-3 P.M.

Ms. Mills. (I call her Sergeant Mills, though never to her face!) But I think that even if we had a normal PE class, I'd probably still **HATe iT**. I don't see the point of running around in the cold, playing hockey or dodgeball or any other sport where people from your own team are getting in your way. Also, I really don't like having to use the gym showers. **UGH!** Just think of all the things you

could catch! Think of the diseases, the nits, the **FUNGi!**

I also don't like having to make small talk with people while I'm changing clothes.

Now, don't get me **WRONG**, I'm not saying that I don't like sports. I like running, climbing and archery. Most of these are things that you do on your own, true, but that's not why I like them. I mean, I'm not bad at other, *group* sports. It's just that I sometimes get **carried away** and … well … people get hurt. It's just safer for everyone involved if **I STEER CLEAR OF GROUP SPORTS**.

**19**

Anyway, as I was saying, math had been **canceLLed**, but we still had PE after lunch. The healthy eating talks were being held in the assembly hall and the whole of our year had to attend. Holly was really excited. She came up to me and said, "**HURRY UP!** I want to get a seat near the Trumpmaster G!" (That's what she calls the teacher's pet, Gareth Trumpshaw.)

*"Everything you've just said is ridiculous. I really don't understand what you see in him."* That's what I wanted to say. Of course,

that's not what I said. What I actually said was: "Sure Holly, lead the way. Can you just remind me again what it is that you see in him?"

"Well, he's really **SMART** and he **DRESSES REALLY WELL** ..." said Holly with a smile.

I thought for a moment. "But we're in school—we have a uniform. Don't you think he dresses just like everyone else?"

Holly laughed. "No, silly! Some people just wear their uniform with style. He's got great hair and he smells

**WONDERFUL**."

I was going to reply with something

**sarcastic**, but then I stopped to think. I mean,

if those things are important to you and you

compare Gareth to other boys in his class, I can

see her point. **LOOK AT DANNY**

**AND PERCY!** I don't think Danny's

shirt has **EVER** seen an iron and Percy

only manages to put his sweater on the right

way around half of the time. (Everyone says it's

because he's a bit dim, but I think it is clearly

because he's got far deeper worries.) And as

far as the smell, true: most of the boys in our

school **DO** smell. It's like a combination of old socks and pickled onion chips, apart from Danny who smells a bit like **TOAD**.

"Okay," I said, "I'll give you that. He's a bit **LESS GRIMY** than the other boys in the year, but what about his personality?"

Holly looked at me blankly. **"WHAT PERSONALITY?"**

"Don't you think he's a bit stuck up and full of himself? I mean, do you want a **NICE BOYFRIEND** you have something in common with, or just someone who would

**25**

look good in a **SHAMPOO COMMERCIAL?**"

Holly gasped and clutched my arm. "Oh my god! Can you imagine how cool that would be? Like, if he were a **FAMOUS**

model on a shampoo advert and I could be, like, his assistant. **I COULD WASH HiS HAiR!!!**"

"Okay," I told her, "I guess that would be quite cool." I lied—I really didn't know what to reply to that; it's the saddest thing I've ever heard! (Well okay, maybe not the **SADDEST**... but it's close!)

Anyway, we made it to the assembly hall and Holly made a beeline for Gareth. But instead of sitting next to him, she sat in the row in front of him, just off to his right.

"I thought you wanted to sit *next*

to Gareth, you know, **SO YOU COULD TALK TO HiM** ..."

I whispered as I sat beside her.

Holly gave me a funny look. "I'm not going to actually talk to him, don't you know anything? I'm just going to sit where

he can see me. Just in front of him and to the right so if I turn around, he can see my left side. That's my pretty-but-shy side."

"Of course, that makes sense," I replied, nodding. Seriously though, that makes **NO SeNSe!** Not to me, anyway. I sometimes think that Holly is either one sandwich short of a picnic, or she's some kind of evil genius.

Holly turned to give Gareth an **innocent smiLe** and he smiled right back at us. Then she pretended not to notice him as she twiddled her hair around a pencil.

Holly really seems to know something about boys that I don't. Maybe she **iS** an **eViL GeNiuS**. In any case, I was glad when the healthy eating talk started.

Mr. Norton the headmaster took the stage, but nobody seemed to take much **NOTiCe**.

"Settle down everybody!" he said.

Nobody did.

He raised his voice, "Children, settle down or you'll all be staying late."

Nothing.

He yelled, "Children, shut up right now or you'll all be doing double PE!"

Finally, silence.

Mr. Norton cleared his throat. "Okay everybody, now before the talk starts, let me remind you all that the **CHARiTY FUN RUN** is coming up. You can all get your sponsor forms from my secretary Miss Austin. You can either go and see her in her office, or you can email her at *greenville_admin@yoo-hoo.com.*"

"Right," he continued, "on to the talk! As you may all know, the Western world has a growing public health problem. We're eating **TOO MUCH** of the wrong sort of food and not getting enough exercise. If we carry on like this, you'll all get diabetes and your teeth will fall out. Oh, and your livers will implode."

**WHAT?**

Mr. Norton glanced over at Miss Quimby, one of the teachers in our year who is famous for her love of **DONUTS**. She was standing in the back corner of the hall munching on a donut.

Miss Quimby was a **PERFECT** example of what Mr. Norton was talking about. I'm not in her class, but Percy is. He says that sometimes she bends down behind her desk pretending to be looking for something and when she gets back up, she has **CHOCOLATE** in the corners of her mouth. He also told me that she has so many fillings that she sets off the alarms at airport security. But I think he may have made that one up.

"Anyway," said Mr. Norton, bringing my attention back to his speech, "we've brought in an expert to teach you all about healthy eating. **PLEASE WELCOME MR. WILLIAMS!**"

A cheerful looking man with stubble and curly hair made his way **CLUMSILY** onto the stage. One or two people clapped, and Mr. Williams looked out toward us like a man on an **ALL-IMPORTANT MISSION**.

"Hello, I'm Mr. Williams and I'm here to tell you about **HeALTHY eATiNG**. We're going to talk about different foods and we're going to put them into two categories called **FOOD FRieNDS** and **FOOD FOeS**. Now, who here likes broccoli?"

Mr. Williams searched the audience with his eyes but he was met with a deadly silence. This didn't seem to put him off, though; this clearly wasn't his first tough audience.

"Well, did you know that broccoli is really good for you?" he continued. "We're going to go ahead and put **BROCCOLi** under **FOOD FRieNDS**."

He made his way toward a big whiteboard at the back of the stage. It had a big black line down the middle making two sections, one with the heading '**FOOD FRieNDS**' and one with the heading '**FOOD Foes**'. He scribbled the word broccoli under Food Friends in really small writing. I was hit by a sudden sinking feeling. If he was going to fill up the whole whiteboard, we were in for a

**very Long and very boring TaLk**.

Mr. Williams turned to face us again. "What about pizza, good or bad for you?"

Again, he was met with a deadly silence. He decided to start singling people out. "You!" he said, pointing to Holly.

"Er ... bad?" Holly replied.

Mr. Williams beamed. **"EXCELLENT!** Pizza is a Food Foe. Now, what about sprouts?"

You get the idea. By the end of the

**VERY LONG** talk we had a list

of Food Friends that included **broccoLi,**

**sprouts, onions, eggs, Lean meat, miLk,**

**beans, rice, fruit, tomatoes, fish,** etc.

FOOD
FRiENDS

And a list of Food Foes like **pizza, burgers, chicken nuggets, chips, French fries, cookies, fried food, chocolate, and candy.**

**FOOD FOES**

Mr. Williams also told us to **avoid snacking** too much between meals, that we should be careful with our portion sizes, and that we should all get plenty of **exeRcise**. So, nothing that we didn't know already.

When we finally reached the end of the talk, Mr. Williams looked around and said, "Just before we finish, does anyone have **ANY QUESTIONS?**"

I looked around the room. Everyone looked **HALF ASLeeP**, so I lifted my hand.

43

44

Mr. Williams looked at me blankly, then the school bell rang.

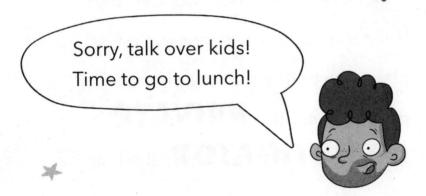

Sorry, talk over kids!
Time to go to lunch!

It was one of the rare days that I was actually looking forward to lunch, but that probably had something to do with the fact that I'd just spent the last hour listening to a talk about food. Even Holly's endless chat about dancing and handbags wasn't going to put me off my food.

I know a lot of people wonder why Holly and I are even friends in the first place. The truth is that Holly is the perfect friend for a **PRIVATE INVESTIGATOR**: she has

absolutely no interest in anything I do and therefore she never finds out about the cases I'm **INVESTIGATING**. And I'm the perfect friend for Holly because I'm usually happy to go along with whatever she wants to do, so it works out well for both of us.

Holly has been going to dance lessons since she was about three, which is pretty impressive. I mean, it's hard work and exercise and it takes discipline. The thing is that she's really **OBSESSED** with becoming a celebrity. All she ever talks about is wanting to be a famous pop star.

This morning, she spent an hour telling me about all the **DiFFERENT** clothes she'll need when she grows up and goes on tour. Then she said, "But don't worry, when I'm **famous** I won't let it go to my head—I'll still remember the little people ... **HEY!** I've had a great idea! When I'm famous, you could work for me as my personal shopper! Wouldn't it be great?! We could spend all day going from shop to shop. You could watch me try on **COOL OUTFITS** and tell me which ones look the best."

I did feel a bit insulted that:

a) Holly doesn't seem to know or care about how much I **HATE** shopping.

b) Holly doesn't seem to know or care about what I want to do when *I grow up*.

c) Holly just referred to me as 'the little people'.

On the other hand, I couldn't help thinking what fun it could be to advise her on some 'cool outfits' …

As we were lining up with our lunch

trays, I could hear Holly behind me going

# ON AND ON

about her plans, "Of

course, if I'm going

to audition for

Young Talent,

I'll have to get

the school behind me. They interview your

friends, you know? I'll need everybody to

see me dancing and singing so they can say

things like 'she was born to be a star' and

'she's so talented' … And then, I'll need to

have a really good boyfriend like Gareth who can give it the human angle, you know? Tell everyone what a **great person** I am, that I'm kind to little animals, and how lucky he is to be with someone so **pretty** and so **clever** ..."

"Young Talent?" I asked. "What's that?"

Holly looked at me with a mix of shock and disgust. "Have you been living under a rock? It's only, like, the **MOST** important talent contest **ever!**

"You audition and then, if they pick you, they train you to be part of a band. **AND** the whole thing is on TV so you become, like, **SUPER FAMOUS!**"

"And you're auditioning for Young Talent?" I asked.

She looked at me as if I hadn't really been paying attention. She was right: I hadn't been paying attention at all.

"Not yet, silly," she said. "I need to get the whole school behind me first. Anyway, I'm too busy training for the **charity fun run**."

I was surprised. It wasn't like Holly to willingly get sweaty in front of people. "Really? What's the charity?"

"Oh, good point!" said Holly. "What charity? I'd better find out! I'm just doing it because it's **GOOD PUBLiCiTY**, but I probably should find out what charity I'm doing it for. I mean, I don't want to look completely stupid if I get interviewed by the press!"

I had to admire Holly. I mean, sure, she may sometimes seem amazingly shallow, but she's an amazingly shallow girl with a **PLAN!**

"Anyway," Holly continued, "you should know all about the fun run. You're doing it too."

That came as a bit of a surprise.

"Am I? Since when?"

Holly gave me a funny look. "**DUH!** Since nobody wanted to enter and Ms. Mills made us all sign up. You can only get out of it if you have some other school event. You have to get your friends and family to sponsor you too. All the money goes to a **good cause**."

This was news to me; I obviously hadn't been paying attention in the last PE class. But at least it meant that we'd be running in PE class. **I LiKe RUNNiNG**.

Holly and I made our way through the line and found a table to sit at. Holly had just moved the topic on to sequined leg warmers when I looked down at my tray: **CHICKEN-NUGGET PIZZA**. For dessert there was a dollop of ice cream on a bed of sprinkles, and smothered in chocolate sauce. It was all to be washed down with an **EXTRA** fizzy cola topped with **MARSHMALLOWS**.

I took a deep breath and interrupted Holly's fashion report. "Um, Holly ... have you looked at my tray?"

Holly looked down. Then she looked back at me, a bit puzzled. "Looks normal, is there a **BUG** on it or something?"

"Have you looked at the food?"

Holly took another look. For a brief moment she forgot all about leg warmers. "Hang on a minute," she said, "aren't all of these things **FOOD FOES?** I thought the school was supposed to be **encouraging healthy eating**."

Holly might be a bit shallow, but she's not stupid.

"Exactly," I nodded. "That's *exactly* what I was thinking."

Holly opened her lunch box and pulled out a **chicken saLad**. "I'm really glad I bring my own lunch," she said airily. "I mean can you imagine what *that* would do to my fitness program?

I need to be in perfect shape if I'm going to be a **POP STAR**, you know. All that dancing is hard work."

"Right … do you remember what I had yesterday?"

Holly frowned. "Was it a **doubLe cheeseburger** and **raspberry-rippLe ice cream?**"

"Yes, and the day before that?"

"No idea."

I looked at her grimly. "Just a giant plate of **French fries** covered in ketchup and melted cheese."

# "GROSS!"

"… with a **slice of chocolate cake**." I thought for a minute. **"I wonder why none of the teachers have said anything?"**

Holly looked around and leaned in to me as if to reveal a **BiG SeCReT**.

"I think a lot of them bring their own food."

She was right! The only teacher who regularly ate the cafeteria food was Miss Quimby and, to her, lunch was just a light snack between boxes of **donuts**.

The more I thought about it, the stranger it seemed: why would the school encourage healthy eating yet give us all really unhealthy lunches? Something didn't add up. Somebody was hiding something.

# THIS SOUNDED LIKE A CASE FOR MINA MISTRY.

# LOG ENTRY #2

Location: Granny Meera's house
Status: Enjoying spending the whole
weekend with Granny Meera

Quite a lot has happened over the past

couple of days, so I think it's time to catch

up. When I got home on Friday, I found

I was **HOME ALONE**. Mom

is away all month inspecting a factory in

Bangladesh, and I found a **NOTE** from Dad on the fridge:

Dear Mina,

I'll be away all weekend. I have to work. Sorry! I have a secret mission I know you understand. Granny Meera will pick you up later, you're spending the weekend with her.

Be good. I love you!

Dad

The note didn't come as much of a surprise—Dad often has to go away on **SECRET MISSIONS**. Dad *says* he works for the ministry of transport, but I know that this is just a cover. He is really a spy. I mean, I don't know for sure because obviously he's not allowed to tell me, but it's pretty obvious.

I've come to this conclusion based on the information in his personal file.

# PERSONAL FILE:

**Name:** Charles Snotbridge

**Occupation:** Spy (his cover story is that he works for the Ministry of Transport)

**Distinguishing Features:** Medium height, medium build, light brown hair, brown eyes, scruffy beard. In summary: he doesn't have any distinguishing features. (This is clue number one that he's a spy.)

He has to look as normal as possible so he doesn't stand out in a crowd)

**Hobbies:** Playing with his model trains in the attic and spying on neighbors with his telescope. (He pretends he's into astronomy, but he can't fool me, I know that there's no such constellation as 'The Giant Slug'. Also, he always seems to know things like 'Mrs. Gibson just bought a new lawnmower' or 'Next door's cat has just been sick on Mr. Nesbit's doorstep'.)

It's a shame Dad wasn't in. He would have been the perfect person to talk to about the mystery of the **disgustingLy unheaLthy schooL Lunches**. On the other hand, at least I got to spend the weekend with Granny Meera! I stay with Granny Meera quite a lot. In fact, I've got my own bedroom at her house.

Granny Meera is **GReAT**. She's my mom's mom. She doesn't like my dad much, so she pretends that she can't speak English very well. We all go along with it, even though she's not really fooling anyone.

Granny Meera has her own special brand of **fusion cooking**. She loves mixing traditional English food with traditional Indian food. It's a bit hit-and-miss. Her **onion-bahjis-in-the-hole** are a **DEFINITE HIT** (you can't do that much harm by

adding batter to batter), but I can't say the same for her **fish fingers with Peshawari naan**. That's all part of the fun though, you never know what you're going to get.

Anyway, like I said, Granny Meera doesn't like Dad very much. Dad thinks that it's because she knows that he doesn't like her cooking. This isn't helped by the fact that whenever Dad is around her, he tries to impress her by eating whatever she makes and pretending to like it. Granny Meera still hasn't forgotten the time that she was about to put Molly's dog food down when

Dad walked in, took a spoonful and declared, 'Wow Meera, this is your most **deLicious recipe** yet!'

Granny Meera does **NOT** like the fact that Dad can't tell the difference between her cooking and dog food. Plus, she's still upset about the fact that when Mom and Dad were dating, Dad accidentally ran his car over her **POODLe**. Fortunately, Molly recovered, but Granny Meera's opinion of Dad never did.

# PERSONAL FILE:

**Name:** Granny Meera

**Occupation:** Part-time caterer, has a small business called Cooking con Fusion (she says that's how you say fusion cooking in Spanish)

**Best Friend:** Molly, her poodle

**Distinguishing Features:** Short and plump with gray hair worn up in a bun. Very thick glasses.

**Hobbies:** Inventing recipes

Even if Dad doesn't, I love Granny Meera. She always thinks of **FUN** activities for Mr. Panda to do.

I took Dad's note off the fridge and made myself a sandwich. Then I went up to my room to write in my diary and talk to Mr. Panda about

# WHITe-WATeR RAFTiNG.

Granny Meera picked us up in her **neon yeLLow van** that evening. I'd packed a bag with a few clothes for me and a couple of extreme sports magazines for Mr. Panda. I don't need to take much stuff, though. My room at Granny Meera's house is already full of clothes and books and things.

Granny Meera beamed at me as I clambered into the van. I made sure that Mr. Panda was tucked safely into my backpack before putting on my seatbelt. Granny Meera is a bit of a daredevil on the road.

"I'm so happy you're staying over this weekend, Pumpkin, I could really use your help," she said as she put her foot down and **VIOLENTLY** pulled out of our little lane and onto the main road. She missed a swerving delivery van by inches.

I smiled from ear to ear; I knew just what this meant. Granny Meera wanted my help with **COOKiNG AND BAKiNG**.

I really enjoy cooking with Granny Meera. I like being useful and spending time with her. And I especially like the fact that she lets me carry out the most **BiZARRe** food

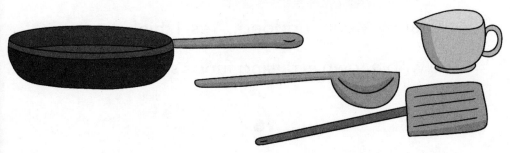

experiments, and then she serves them to people—no matter how bad they taste!

"You know I'm always happy to help, Gran. What's the occasion this time?" I said.

"I'm making **sandwiches and finger food** to sell at the community fundraiser," said Granny Meera. "Haven't you heard about it? The whole town is involved."

I had a think …

"Does this have anything to do with the school charity fun run?"

Granny Meera nodded. "Yes, I think so. The whole town is raising funds so we can help **poor Postman Pete** get back on his feet. He was **BiTTeN** by that awful Yorkshire Terrier on Grimble Street when he was doing his post round."

I frowned. "Didn't that happen ages ago when he **LOST HiS ARM?**"

"No, dear," said Granny Meera, "he lost his arm to an Alsatian, completely different breed. This time, he got his jacket sleeve caught in a mailbox. The owners' Yorkshire Terrier was playing in the garden at the time, but he must have thought that Postman Pete was trying to **break in**. While Pete was wrestling with the mailbox, the dog ran up to him and **BiT HiM ON THE BUM**."

I went a bit quiet. I was trying to work out why Postman Pete getting bitten by a dog was going to require the whole town to raise funds for him.

"So what are we raising funds for exactly? New trousers for Postman Pete? How expensive can that be?"

"Oh, no, dear," Granny Meera continued. "The problem is that after the Yorkshire Terrier bit Pete on the bum, the dog got very sick. The owners **cLaĪmed** that Pete's bum had given their dog food poisoning, so they sued him. Now the poor man has no money left. Anyway, tomorrow there's a fundraiser fair with a rummage sale and games, and next week there's going to be a **sponsored run**—all to raise money for Pete."

I shrugged. "Well, it sounds like a **FUN WEEKEND**, especially if it's all for a good cause. Can you sponsor me in the fun run, by the way?"

"Of course, dear!" she said. "If you help me out

## VILLAGE FESTIVAL

### RUMMAGE SALE, GAMES AND A SPONSORED RUN

To raise money for Postman Pete!

with my cooking, I'll sponsor you for, let's say, ten pounds?"

I grinned at her. "Thanks, Gran! That's great!"

Granny Meera **SLAMMED** on the brakes as we pulled into her driveway and the van **SCREECHED** to a halt. We jumped out of the van and headed for the front door. Granny Meera opened it quietly. Molly the poodle was **cowering** in the corner, as she still does every time she hears a car in the driveway. She has done that ever since that incident with Dad.

"Hello, Molly! Look who's here!" said Granny Meera cheerfully.

Molly limped cautiously over to the door. When she saw me, she started wagging her tail and hopping up and down. I think she likes it when we stay over: Molly and Mr. Panda get on very well.

I left Mr. Panda in the living room to
have a chat with Molly and took my bag
to my room. Then I went back out to the
van to help Granny Meera unload the
**SUPPLieS**.

There were **mangoes,** bags of different spices, yogurt, **Stilton cheese**, Cheddar cheese, chicken, rice, onions, garlic, coconut milk, **baked beans**, spinach … this was going to be interesting. When we finished putting things away, Granny Meera made us both a **CUP OF CARDAMOM COCOA** (a classic hit). We sat in the kitchen as she explained the menu to me. Some of her ideas sounded like they might really work, but some of them

**85**

sounded absolutely awful. I couldn't wait!

Once we'd finished planning in the kitchen, we all curled up together in the living room to watch the wrestling.

I woke up on Saturday morning to the **smeLL of cooking**. I knew that Granny Meera had probably been up for hours. I got ready and went downstairs to see what I could help with. I popped my head around the living room door to say good morning to Mr. Panda and Molly. They were sat on the **SOFA WATCHiNG TV**.

I made my way to the kitchen where Granny Meera had **BEEN VERY BUSY**. There were pies and trays of food **EVERYWHERE**.

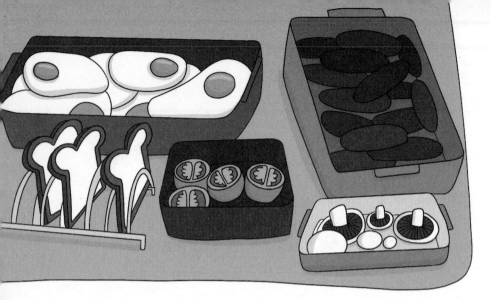

Granny Meera smiled as I walked in.

"**Good morning, Pumpkin**, did you sleep well? Put on your hairnet and have a seat. I've made you a full English breakfast."

I sat at the kitchen table and Granny Meera brought me my breakfast. I saw that there were several trays of **sausages, eggs, fried tomatoes, mushrooms and toast**.

Yes, dear. The rest is going in the samosas. Did you see Mr. Panda and Molly? They've been up for hours. I left them in the living room watching the snooker.

Yes, I said good morning.

As I tucked into my breakfast, one of my teeth **TWINGED** in protest. I put my toast down and read the menu that Granny Meera had written out on a whiteboard on the kitchen wall.

## SANDWICHES:

Cheddar cheese and mango chutney

Tangy roast chicken with mushroom chutney

## FINGER FOOD:

Full English breakfast samosas

## PIES:

Steak and kidney vindaloo

Shepherd's saag paneer pie

## TARTS:

Baked bean biryani quiche

Tandoori chicken and lentil custard

## DESSERTS:

Sticky toffee pudding masala

Coconut and cardamom scones

I had to admit, some of that **sounded decent**. "That all looks really good, Gran, far better than anything that we get in school. **WHAT CAN I HELP YOU WITH?**"

Granny Meera took a tray of scones out of the oven and stopped to look at the whiteboard.

"Well, let's see … I've made the **pies** and the **desserts**, so all that's left to do is fill the sandwiches and samosas, and make the tarts. **WOULD YOU LIKE TO TRY A SCONE?**"

"No thanks, Gran, I have a bit of a pain in one of my teeth. I think I might need a filling," I said.

"Oh dear! We'd better get you an appointment with Dr. Austin, the dentist. We'll do it today. Apparently she has quite a long waiting list, so don't let me forget!"

I wasn't really surprised that Dr. Austin had a long waiting list: **everyone** at school seemed to have tooth trouble. There was always somebody **COMPLAINING ABOUT A TOOTHACHE**.

I nodded at Granny Meera as
I cleared my plate away. Granny
Meera prepared an area where
we could make the sandwiches.

"Okay, Pumpkin, I see you're wearing
your hairnet. **NOW, WASH
YOUR HANDS** ..." she began.

"... and put on an apron and gloves," I
finished, *rolling my eyes*. "Yes, I know."

"That's right, dear. Now, you make
the **Cheddar and mango chutney
sandwiches**, and I'll make the other ones."

Granny Meera laid the ingredients out

in front of me. I gave a sniff. **"THIS ALL SMELLS GREAT, GRAN!"**

Granny Meera looked pleased. "Thank you, dear, I always find that the secret is to use **good-quality, fresh ingredients**."

"I wish you were the cook at our school," I continued. It was true: it would be **HeALTHieR** and

it would definitely be entertaining. I had a vision of Miss Quimby biting into one of Granny Meera's **fire-hot cauliflower donuts**. They look totally innocent until you realize that the sprinkles are actually insanely hot chili flakes.

"Why? What's wrong with the food at school?" Granny Meera asked.

"Oh, it's just **AWFUL**

… It's all junk food, Gran," I said.

"Everything is fatty or sweet, or both. I

don't understand it: they're always going

on about healthy eating, but all we get is

**PiZZA AND DeSSeRT**."

Granny Meera looked up from her

sandwiches. "That's strange,"

she said. She pointed her

spoon at me and a dollop

of mushroom chutney

catapulted past my

ear and landed

on the pantry door. "Isn't your school cook Helen Mudge?"

It rang a bell. "Um, yes, I think so?"

"Well that's funny," said Granny Meera, "because I used to work with Helen. She was a **very good cook**, and was always worried about **healthy eating**. I can't imagine what could have made her change her mind. Maybe you should speak to her."

I thought about it. "Hmm, maybe. Okay, sandwiches finished. What's next?"

Granny Meera looked at the whiteboard. "Okay, the next thing is the

# ENGLISH BREAKFAST SAMOSAS."

I looked over at the trays of **sausages, fried eggs, mushrooms, fried tomatoes and buttered toast.** Next to them sat the tiny pastry squares we were supposed to fill.

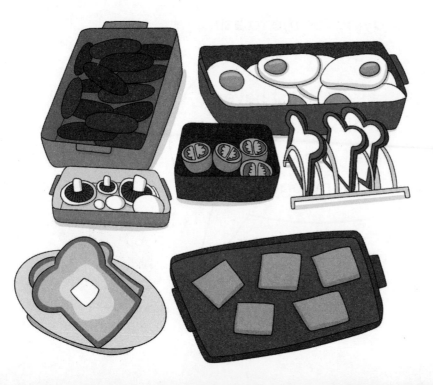

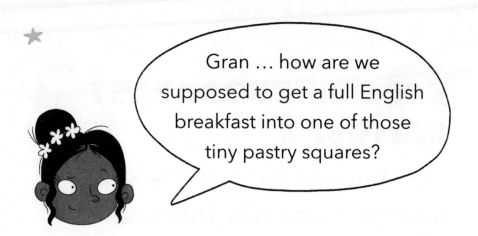

Gran … how are we supposed to get a full English breakfast into one of those tiny pastry squares?

Granny Meera looked at me like she'd been dying for me to ask.

Easy! We just have to make all the pieces really small and mix them together.

How?

In the blender. Just pop all the ingredients in the blender, mix them into a smooth, mushy goo, add a bit of garam masala and there you go!

I had a feeling this was not going to be one of Granny Meera's most successful recipes. I decided I'd try the **samosas** last.

**101**

After that all we have left to do is fill the tarts. You can do the baked bean biryani ones while I finish making the lentil custard.

Lentil custard?

Yes, it's a secret recipe. Well, it's not that I keep it a secret, it's just that nobody ever seems to want it.

102

I changed my mind. I'd be trying the **LENTIL CUSTARD** last (if at all).

Although I enjoyed scooping **baked bean biryani** out of a bowl and splodging it into the tarts, my mind was on other things. Why were the school lunches so unhealthy?

If Mrs. Mudge knew how to make **good food**, then she had to be doing this on purpose. I was going to have to interrogate her. **I HAD MY FiRST SUSPECT.**

Normally I would go up to my room and have a secret meeting with Mr. Panda. He always advises me on how to carry out my investigations. Unfortunately, my bedroom at Granny Meera's is right next to her room and I couldn't risk anyone overhearing our discussion. This meant Mr. Panda and I had to hold our **secret meeting in the shed.**

I waited until Granny Meera had fallen asleep in her armchair watching the wrestling, then Mr. Panda and I met in the shed.

First of all, we went over the facts:

We knew that the school was in favor of serving healthy meals, but it wasn't happening. Somebody was **INTERFERING** with the school meals.

But why?

The most obvious motivation seemed to be money. Was somebody at the school making money from doing this and, if so, how?

According to Granny Meera, fresh food isn't necessarily more expensive than processed food. So I don't think anyone would be **SAVING MONEY** by buying processed food instead of fresh food. We had another think ... **COULD THE SUPPLIER BE IN ON IT?**

Maybe the food supplier and Mrs. Mudge were working together. **Maybe Mrs. Mudge knew the supplier.** If she bought all the food for the school exclusively from them, the supplier in turn might give her part of the profits. **IT SEEMED TO MAKE SENSE.**

Mr. Panda insisted that the next step would be to

**INTERROGATE** Mrs. Mudge. It would have to be during the school day. We discussed it some more and came up with a plan.

# LOG ENTRY #3

Location: My bedroom

Status: Putting the plan into action

I went straight to school from Granny Meera's this morning, all set to put Mr. Panda's **PLAN** into motion.

I needed to speak to Mrs. Mudge, the cook. I knew I wouldn't be able to do it at **Lunchtime** as she'd be too busy, but we had

PE during second period and I knew just **HOW TO GET OUT OF IT**.

I knew that we'd be running during most of the class. All I had to do was **PRETEND** to trip up and fall, then I could get Ms. Mills to give me permission to go and see the nurse. On my way there I could accidentally 'get lost' and end up in the school kitchen … **PIECE OF CAKE!**

I took my place on the running track and waited for Ms. Mills to blow her whistle. The easiest way to fake the fall would be to stay in the middle of the group, so that no one could really see what happened. I didn't have to wait for long. We'd been running for about a minute when I noticed that Ms. Mills seemed distracted. I threw myself

# DRAMATICALLY ON THE FLOOR.

I heard someone shout 'Runner down!' and then **FEET TRAMPLING ALL AROUND ME**. I'm pretty sure that a few people jumped over me.

Then Ms. Mills screamed, "**KEEP RUNNING YOU LOT!** What are you looking at?"

She came over to me. "Are you alright, Mina?"

"Erm, I don't know … **OW! …**

# IT'S MY ANKLE ... I think

I might have sprained it." I got up so she could see me hobble around in pain. "I think I'd better go to see the nurse."

Sadly, Ms. Mills was far too convinced by my excellent acting skills. "Yes, well," she said, "you won't be able to walk there on your own. I'll take you."

**RATS!** I hadn't counted on that. Ms. Mills left Holly in charge of the class whilst she helped me shuffle slowly toward the nurse's office. **I was doomed.** Not only would I not get to sneak off and interrogate

Helen Mudge, but the nurse would tell Ms. Mills that there was nothing wrong with my ankle. I was going to be in **BiG** trouble.

The hallway seemed to narrow in front of my eyes as we made the long shuffle toward the nurse's office. We were just around the corner ... **THEN SUDDENLY, A MiRACLE HAPPENED!**

Mr. Hammond, the science teacher came around the corner on his way to the coffee machine. Ms. Mills has a **HUGE CRUSH** on Mr. Hammond but I'm pretty sure he's as terrified of her as we are. He looked startled as he came face to face with her.

Ms. Mills suddenly let go of my arm and said, "There you go, dear. It's just around the corner."

She pointed me toward the end of the hallway and I breathed a **sigh of relief**.

Ms. Mills turned to chase Mr. Hammond down the hallway. That had been a close one! I shuffled carefully around the corner, then **BOLTED** toward the school kitchens.

I could hear talking and **smell cooking**. The talking seemed to be coming from the delivery bay at back of the kitchen. I crouched down by a fridge **AND TRIED TO LISTEN IN**.

I could hear Mrs. Mudge, the cook,

talking to a delivery driver. She did NOT sound happy.

"I can't believe it's happened again! This is not the order I placed, where are my peppers? **WHERE ARE ALL THE FRESH INGREDIENTS I ORDERED?**"

"Look, I don't know what you're talking about!" the delivery driver said grumpily. "This is the order that the school sent through, look: **50 BOXES OF FROZEN PIZZA, 50**

# BOXES OF CHICKEN NUGGETS, AND 10 TUBS OF TRIPLE CHOCOLATE ICE CREAM.

Look at the email address at the top. It *says:*

*greenville_admin@yoo-hoo.com."*

"*I just don't understand it,*" Mrs. Mudge *sighed, "that's Mr. Norton's secretary. I can't believe that Mr. Norton, the headmaster of this very school—*man who is supposed to be promoting **healthy eating**—would change my order for **junk food**."

**BiNGO!!** It looked like I wouldn't even need to interrogate–I mean interview–Helen Mudge after all. We had a new suspect: **MR. NORTON**.

Hmm, investigating Mr. Norton was going to be a bit more complicated. I didn't know where to begin. Who knows what headmasters get up to all day? I was going to have to find a way to catch him out. Maybe if I could find a way of making a food order myself, I could see what was going on ... But first I had to get out of the kitchen without being seen.

I backed away from the fridge and sneaked toward the kitchen door. I crept backward out through it, but stepped into a puddle of something **SLiMY** that sent me flying!

I got quickly to my feet. Fortunately no one had seen me. On standing up, though, I realized that I'd *actually* sprained my ankle …

# OW!!!

I hobbled down the hallway to the nurse's office. I guess this was my punishment for **FAKiNG AN iNJURY!** I knocked on the nurse's door.

"Just a minute!" she called. I waited for a couple of minutes, then Percy came out looking pale and sweaty and the nurse told me to come in. She examined me and confirmed that I had a **sprained ankle**. She bandaged it up with a bit of elastic bandage and told me not to put too much weight on it.

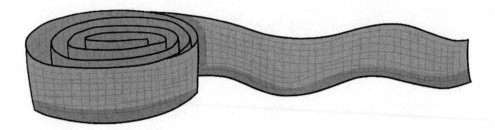

I asked if I would be able to take part in the fun run at the weekend.

"I don't think so," she said. "You shouldn't do any exercise for a couple of weeks."

**RATS!** *I really wanted to do that run. I like running*—I usually come in first. And I wanted to help raise funds for Postman Pete, too.

"Oh well, look on the bright side," the nurse continued, "at least you get out of PE for a couple of weeks. Now, back to class with you, and be careful in the hallway—**PERCY HAS JUST BEEN SICK ON THE FLOOR**."

**126**

When I got home from school this afternoon, Dad's car was in the driveway. I **hobbLed** up two flights of stairs to the attic where I knew he'd either be playing with his model trains or **SPYING ON THE NEIGHBORS** through his telescope.

Dad's railway model is **REALLY IMPRESSIVE** and very realistic. It's an exact replica of our town. It takes up most of the attic. Thank goodness Greenville isn't a very big place!

As I pushed open the attic door, I could see Dad looking for a part for his railway model in one of his numbered boxes.

Dad looked up. "**MINA!** How are you, darling?" Then he did a double take. "What happened to your leg?"

"Oh, don't worry," I said. "It's nothing, just a little sprain. How was work?"

Dad tapped his nose. "You know I can't discuss that ... **TOP SECRET!**"

I approached the telescope by the window and peered through it.

129

Dad found the part he was looking for.
He went to get some glue from his desk,
then he glued a tiny little satellite dish onto
the roof of the replica of the Robinsons'
house on his model.

"How was school?" he asked.

I tapped my nose. "I can't tell you, **iT'S TOP SeCReT**."

Dad smiled at my joke.

"Actually," I said, "there's going to be a fun run at the weekend to raise funds for Postman Pete. I was going to ask you to sponsor me, but it would be more of a sponsored limp."

"That's alright, darling, I'll still sponsor you." He frowned. "Oh, that reminds me! Holly called for you. She said that her internet is down and that she needs you to email the school secretary to get her sponsor form for the fun run."

"Oh okay, thanks, Dad. Actually, I was thinking that after the fun run it might be nice for the school to throw a party for

Postman Pete. And, as the school

is campaigning for **heaLthy**

**eating**, I thought it would

be good if we designed a

menu of **HEALTHY**

**SNACKS**."

"Ah yes, poor Pete," Dad said.

He looked down at his model

of the town. In the garden of

number 52 Grimble Street you

could see a tiny model dog with its

teeth bared.

"I'm sure Pete would love that," Dad

continued, "and I'm sure your grandmother

could help you with the menu."

I nodded. "Great idea, I'll call her!" I

turned toward the door to go.

"Oh wait, Mina ..."

I looked back at him.

"You aren't throwing this party just to cover up the fact you're doing an **UNDERCOVER INVESTIGATION**, are you?"

Dad winked at me and then turned his attention back to his model railway. As I blundered down the stairs I heard him shout, "Don't forget the meteor shower tonight after dinner!"

How did Dad know about my investigation? Mind you, he *is* a spy, so he knows a lot of **SECRETS**.

I found the phone on the coffee table and I called Granny Meera. The first thing she said was that she'd booked me a dentist's appointment. I'd almost forgotten about that! She told me that the earliest appointment with Dr. Austin is in **SiX MONTHS.**

That was strange. "Six months? Isn't there anything sooner?"

"I'm afraid not," replied Granny Meera. "It turns out that there's a **VeRY LONG WAiTiNG LiST**.

Dr Austin is the **ONLY** dentist in town and she's **VERY, VERY BUSY**."

"Okay, thanks, Gran," I replied. "How did the festival go? Was your food a hit?"

"Oh, yes, dear," she said. There was a thoughtful pause. "Mind you, I might have to rethink the recipe for the **LentiL custard**. It's not my best seller. But that teacher from your school, Miss Quimby, bought **aLL oP the scones**."

I was not surprised about Mrs. Quimby and the scones—her sweet tooth was notorious.

"Why don't you leave the lentil custard recipe as it is and just change the name to something like **'CUSTARD SURPRISE'?"** I suggested.

"You're a genius, Pumpkin, what would I do without you?"

I nodded. I *am* a bit of a genius, if I do say so myself. Then I remembered what I'd been meaning to ask. "Anyway Gran, I wanted to ask you a favor. I'm thinking of asking the school to host a party for Postman Pete, could you help me come up with a **HEALTHY MENU?"**

"Of course, Pumpkin," said Granny Meera. "Let me have a think and I'll call you back."

I went up to my room and closed the door. I didn't like bothering Mr. Panda when he was in the middle of reading a rafting magazine, but I knew that he'd want the latest updates on the investigation. I went into my wardrobe and got the **CASe FILe** out from the box

marked **OLD TOYS**. Then I went to

sit with Mr. Panda on the bed.

I started by

updating Mr. Panda

on Helen Mudge's

interview. Well, okay,

it wasn't quite an

interview, more of an

overheard conversation.

Mr. Panda agreed that the next step

would be to **iNVeSTiGATe** Mr.

Norton. He was very interested to hear

about my party idea too.

I'm thinking about asking the school to throw a fundraising party for Postman Pete.

Mr. Panda looked intrigued.

We're already having a fun run so I figured that if the school will let us put on a party, I can volunteer to help Helen Mudge with the food. Then I'll be able to see exactly who it is that's changing the orders.

Mr. Panda thought about it for a bit, then he looked at me **APPROVINGLY**. He said that he liked the idea of the party and the food, but we should put on a bit of a show, too. He thinks it might look less suspicious that way, and it will be easier to get Mr. Norton involved.

I knew he was right. Entertainment wasn't really my area **BUT** I knew someone who could help me out with it. I was going to have to get Holly on board.

**OH! HOLLY!** I suddenly remembered that she needed me to email the school secretary. I opened my email account and started typing the email. Suddenly, I had a realization. I slammed my laptop shut and turned to Mr. Panda.

Mr. Panda! I have some new information that you're going to want to hear!

# LOG ENTRY #4

Location: At home
Status: Investigating

Today didn't quite work out as planned. I headed to school a **full half-hour early** to catch Holly before class, but she swept straight past me and locked herself in a toilet stall to conduct her **DAILY BEAUTY ROUTINE**. It's not like Holly to leave the house without doing

her hair, nails and makeup. Usually she

strolls up to the school doors

like an actress cruising

down a **red carpet**, so I

assumed that she'd had an

argument with her mom.

It wouldn't be the first

time that Holly had upset

her mom by spending

all her birthday money on

makeup. There are lots of

things that Holly and her mom

don't see eye to eye on, and Holly's need to

turn up to school looking like she's about to

shoot a music video is one of them.

Anyway, I crept carefully up to the

bathroom door. I could hear Holly on

the other side **RUMMAGiNG**

**THROUGH HER**

**MAKeUP BAG** and muttering

things like 'I'll give **HER** inner beauty ...' I

knocked on the stall door, but she just started

aggressively blasting out meditation

music.

Holly emerged looking as **BUBBLY**

**AND PRISTINE** as ever just

as the bell rang for class. **RATS!** I'd

missed my chance.

I waited to speak to Holly all morning.

We had math and then English. I really

wanted to pay attention during math

in case I learned something, and Holly

seemed very absorbed during our

**146**

English class. The teacher was talking about **women writers in history**. Holly spent the **WHOLE CLASS** looking up thoughtfully, then scribbling things down.

I had to wait until lunchtime to talk to her. By that time I wasn't so worried about making her a part of my plan. I was more **CURIOUS** to find out what she'd found so interesting in English. Holly still seemed **distracted** as we made our way to the cafeteria.

148

Huh?? No, I was just wondering, where did they go shopping? I mean, it wasn't like nowadays when you can just walk down the high street and nip into one shop for your mascara and another for some sparkly socks. They must have really suffered.

Really? Is that all you were thinking about?

No, of course not. I did have a very important thought.

Which was?

Tell me honestly. Do you think I would suit a hat? I just feel like I don't accessorize enough and maybe hats would be a good start.

**150**

It was hard for me to believe I was even having this conversation. I had to choose my next words **VERY CAREFULLY**.

I gave her a serious look and said, "Well, I don't know an awful lot about accessorizing, but I do think that if you're going to accessorize, you should definitely start with something that keeps your brain warm."

Holly waved her hand at me. "Oh, I know fashion has to be **practical** too, but I just can't work out how you combine a hat with the rest of your wardrobe. I mean should the color match your shoes? What if it **cLashes** with your handbag? What styles and fabrics go with a winter coat? Or a summer dress? It's just too much to think about!

I could see that Holly was on the verge of a **FASHiON MeLTDOWN** and I needed her to snap out of it. Also,

I needed to get her on board with my

**PARTY PLAN.**

"Oooh!" I said in my most enthusiastic

voice. "Did you see Gareth this morning?

Was that a new jacket he was wearing?"

Holly suddenly came back down to Earth.

**"OH MY GOODNESS!**
**YES!"** She clutched my hand. "Navy

blue is such a good color on him."

"Do you know if he'll be doing the fun

run on Saturday?"

"I suppose so, I mean, we all have to

do it. Well ... except for you." Holly

**153**

made a face. "**UGH**, I still haven't decided what I'm going to wear."

I don't think you can go wrong with a full suit of armour.

**NO!** I didn't say that. I really wanted to, but I didn't. What I actually said was, "Wouldn't it be great if at the end of the fun run we got the school to throw a party for Postman Pete? You know, we could have **food, music** …"

Suddenly Holly's eyes lit up. "**OH MY GOODNeSS, MiNA!** That is such a **GOOD iDeA**, it could be just like one of

those charity fundraisers they have on
TV with celebrity guest performers with
perfect teeth and **GLAMOROUS
OUTFITS** ..."

I nodded. "**YES, EXACTLY.**
Exactly like that, only nowhere near as
good. And I think we can forget about
the perfect teeth part—especially in this
school."

Holly wasn't listening anymore. The cogs
in her brain were whirring away as she
imagined a **STAR-STUDDED
CHARITY BENEFIT** with

Holly Loafer, the generous and talented star of the whole show at the center of the action. I prodded my marshmallow fritter with a fork as I waited for her to finish. I'd just pushed it completely under the **pool of golden syrup** when Holly said, "**WOW MiNA!** What a great idea we've had! Just think how good it would be for my career to be the star of a **BiG CHARiTY BeNeFiT!** I'll have to put together a big musical number, we'll need **canapés** and a **few guest stars**. We'll sell tickets to whoever wants to attend and the proceeds can go to Postman Pete."

"That all sounds great," I replied. "It is Tuesday today, though, and the party is on Saturday, so I was thinking more along the lines of a **few baLLoons and some sandwiches**."

Holly looked at me as if I were some sort of alien. "Remind me to **NeVeR** let you organize any of my parties."

This comment didn't upset me. I have absolutely **NO iNTEReST** in organizing events. There was one thing I did need to organize though. "Okay," I said, "I'll leave the entertainment to you, but I want to do the menu."

Holly shrugged. "Sure! **No LenfiL cusfard sandwiches**, though … okay?"

"Yes, that's fine," I replied. "Oh, and we'll have to get Mr. Norton to agree to let us have the party and use the **schooL cafeferia** to do the **food**."

"Don't worry about that," Holly said airily. "I'll go and see his secretary after lunch to get an appointment. Consider it done. After all, it's for charity."

Say what you like about Holly, but she does know how to get things done. She was an instrumental part of my plan. I needed her to arrange all the dancing and music and frills because I needed a diversion. The really important part of the plan was going to be the **FOOD**. I would set a trap to catch the culprit red-handed, and now that I was pretty sure who the **CRIMINAL** actually was, it was going to be easy.

Everything was falling into place.

# LOG ENTRY #5

Location: In Holly's bathroom
Status: Making final preparations
for the big day

Okay, tomorrow is the **BiG DAY**.
It's been a busy week, trying to get
all the preparations ready in time. On
Tuesday and Wednesday everything
seemed like **one big chore**, but by

the time the weekend rolled around I was really looking forward to the party. Dad was away again so I arranged to stay with Holly tonight after school so we could run through the **FiNAL ARRANGEMENTS**. Holly's mom was out at a protest and her dad was in the kitchen making dinner, so we sat in the living room going over the **PLANS**.

Holly had worked really hard, firstly on getting Mr. Norton to agree to host the party and secondly on getting the **wHoLe**

**school involved**. Even so, she had to **COMPROMiSe** on a few of her ideas. We just didn't have enough time to organize them. This meant that instead of printing and selling tickets we'd charge a two pounds entry fee at the door.

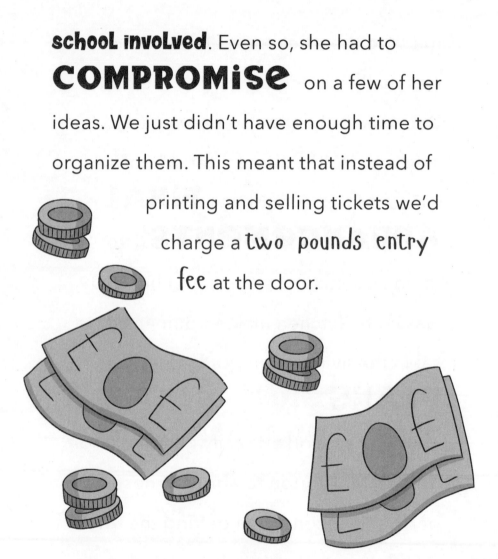

There wasn't enough time for the orchestra to learn Holly's song either. But, luckily, Percy volunteered to accompany her with his homemade one-man-band contraption. Most **DiSAPPOiNTiNGLY** for Holly, we couldn't get a film production crew in to record her performance, so she wouldn't be able to sell DVDs of it. **AS THiNGS STOOD, THE ARRANGEMENTS WERE:**

10:30 – The fun run starts

12:00 – Everyone meets back at the school where there will be a free buffet

12:30 – Meet and greet Postman Pete

12:45 – Entertainment Extravaganza

1:00 – Disco

I was glad to have left the organizing to Holly as it would never have occurred to me to **BOOK A DJ**.

Holly asked Debra Derby from our year to DJ. Apparently, it's important for Holly to have some time to chill out and mingle after her big performance, to speak to 'the little people' and give Gareth Trumpshaw the opportunity to ask her out.

I'd spent the week working on the menu with Granny Meera. This is what we came up with:

Hummus dip with carrot and
celery sticks

Nachos with cheese dip, avocado
dip and spicy tomato dip

Mini sandwiches: Tuna salad,
chicken salad, and ham and mustard

Individual cups of chopped fruit
salad

Fruit punch

Okay, I may have exaggerated a bit there. It didn't take a whole week to come up with that. Mr. Norton agreed that the school would **provide the food**. All I had to do was meet with the cook, take her the menu and make sure she was happy with it.

Helen Mudge was very sweet. She said that she was looking forward to preparing such a **HEALTHY MENU**, and that it

would make a welcome change for her. She also said, "I just hope nothing goes wrong." That's where our opinions differed: I was counting on it going wrong!

Postman Pete had agreed to make a celebrity appearance and pick up his check for the **FUNDS RAISED** to go toward the court case. After that, a few kids from the orchestra had volunteered to play a couple of songs. For the grand finale, Holly was going to sing and do her **LITTLE DANCE NUMBER**.

Holly and I had so much fun organizing the party that I almost forgot what I was doing it for—to solve the mystery of the **LOATHSOME SCHOOL LUNCHES**. Holly, on the other hand, had no doubt why she was doing it.

Once we had finished going over all the details, Holly dragged me up to her room to **ASK ME AN IMPORTANT QUESTION**.

"What's up?" I asked, pulling the door closed behind me.

"Should I go for this **yeLLow sparkLy number**, or is the **red one with the feathers** more me?" said Holly.

I looked at the dresses. "Don't you think you'll be a bit **OVERDRESSED FOR A FUN RUN?**"

Holly laughed. "Don't be silly, it's for my **PERFORMANCE!**"

"I'm not sure it's going to matter if you insist on singing that song you wrote," I replied. "I'm not sure it's very appropriate for a fundraiser. I can't help but feel it's a bit insensitive."

# "OH, DON'T BE SILLY!"

said Holly, "It's about Pete, I'm sure he'll love it … and that Gareth will love me."

I rolled my eyes. "Anyway … After the run I'll meet you at the finish line and you can help me set up the food."

Holly dropped the dress she was holding and looked at me in **DISBELIEF**.

"You don't expect me to finish the run, all **greasy and sweaty**, and start slaving away in the kitchen, **DO YOU? NO WAY!** I'm going home to wash my hair and get ready for my big appearance!"

I suddenly remembered that I was dealing with Holly, Greenville's most important new celebrity. A girl who would **not risk chipping her nail polish for anything in the world**.

"Sorry Holly, what was I thinking? When will you arrive then?"

"I'll arrive **fashionably late**, but in time for my performance—don't worry about that!"

"So who's going to help me with the organization?" I asked.

Holly passed me a **BiNDeR** and I opened it. There was a schedule, a step-by-step explanation of each part of the event and a list of telephone numbers. It was **SURPRiSiNGLY WeLL**

SUPERSTAR
SHOW
SCHEDULE

**ORGANIZED**. I now knew what she'd been doing all week when she was supposed to be paying attention in class.

"Did you arrange for Mr. Norton and his secretary to be there?" I asked.

Holly sighed. "**YES MINA, EVERYTHING'S BEEN DONE**—everyone knows what they have to do. Miss Austin and Mr. Norton will be there to add up the **SPONSOR FORMS AND THE TICKET MONEY**, so we'll know how much we've raised. Amy

**177**

Almond has volunteered to sell tickets at the door and Ms. Mills is going to be the **BOUNCER**. Mr. Norton said that he received your **FOOD ORDER** through to his office so that's all taken care of. All you have to do is put the food out and answer any last-minute questions anyone has.

If you have an **emergency**, text me."

I started to nod. "Hang on ... what do you mean Ms. Mills is going to be the bouncer? You're not expecting **TROUBLE**, are you?"

"Oh, come on!" said Holly. "Every big event needs some security. We don't want too many people trying to clamber in to see my performance."

"If you're going to sing that song, it's going to be more a matter of **STOPPING PEOPLE FROM CLAMBERING OUT**," I replied.

**179**

Holly wasn't listening. As far as she was concerned her job had been done and she seemed **CONFiDeNT** that everything was going to go to plan.

I wasn't so sure.

# LOG ENTRY #6

Location: At home, in bedroom

Status: Putting my master plan into action

It was the day of the investigation/party.

I left Holly's house at about nine a.m. on

Saturday morning. Most of the students and

teachers from Greenville Elementary would

be heading for the fun run. I was sorry to

have to miss it, but I had a lot of work to do.

I went straight to school and made my way

round to the back of the building, where

I'd arranged to meet Helen Mudge by the

door to the kitchen. I rang the bell and

waited to be let in. I was greeted by a very

upset looking Helen Mudge.

"What's wrong, Mrs. Mudge?" I said.

# "OH, MiNA!" SHE CRIED, "IT'S HAPPENED AGAIN!"

I did my best to look confused. "What's

happened again?"

Helen Mudge pointed to a big pile of boxes stacked on a pallet. "I came in early this morning to receive the food delivery and start preparations, but look at what they've delivered: donuts, chips, cookies ..."

# BiNGO! OUR CULPRiT STRiKeS AGAiN!

For a moment I wanted to jump for joy. Everything was going as planned. But then I realized that Mrs. Mudge didn't have a clue about what was going on and she looked **genuineLy upset**. I had to keep

acting as though I didn't know what was happening.

I put my hands on my hips. "This is not the order I sent to Mr. Norton's office!"

"I send all my orders to Mr. Norton too," Mrs. Mudge sighed, "but I never get the food I've asked for. I've been a cook for **THiRTY-FiVe YeARS** and until now I've always been proud of what I do: **heLping kids to grow up strong and heaLthy.**"

She sounded so disappointed. I felt really sorry for her. I decided to try to cheer her up.

"Oh well, don't worry! It is a party, after all, so I'm sure we can make do with this."

Mrs. Mudge and I put everything out onto trays and prepared the buffet. Helen agreed to bring it all out as I had other duties to carry out.

Shortly after we'd finished, a few kids with instruments started arriving. Apparently, Holly had told them to look for me. I went to get Holly's binder and found her schedule:

**10:30** – The fun run starts (Mina setting up catering at school with Mrs. Mudge)

**11:00** – Acts arrive (Mina to help them set up on stage)

**11:45** – Ms. Mills and Amy Almond go to the front door to collect entry fees

**12:00** – Parents and children head back to the school where there will be a free buffet/we start bringing out trays of food

**12:25** – Mina introduces Postman Pete

**12:30** – Speech from Postman Pete

**12:45** – ENTERTAINMENT EXTRAVAGANZA

12:45–12:55 – Bill Crisp and his tuba ('Ode to Joy')

1:00–1:20 – The Greenville Gritlords (popular daytime TV theme tunes)

1:25–1:35 – Holly Loafer's dance show (featuring Percy McDuff's one-man band)

1:40 – Mr. Norton awards Postman Pete his check

1:45 – Debra Derby sets up disco

2:00 – Disco

It was **eLeven a.m**. and the musicians had arrived. So far things were going to plan. In fact, it wasn't long before everyone involved in the organization had turned up and **STARTeD GeTTiNG READY**.

Mr. Norton had come along and was setting up the **sound system**. The musicians were busy tuning their **instruments** and going over their songs.

Amy Almond had even made **posters**. I've glued one in here for reference.

# GREENVILLE ELEMENTARY

## FUNDRAISER SPECIAL

Today at 12:00 p.m.

Buffet, Entertainment

Extravaganza and Disco

# ENTRY: £2

## EVERYONE WELCOME!

### ALL PROCEEDS TO BE DONATED
### TO POSTMAN PETE'S LEGAL FUND

GReeNViLLe ELeMeNTARY

FUNDRAiSeR SPeCiAL

THIS SATURDAY AT 12.00 P.M.
FREE BUFFET, ENTERTAINMENT
EXTRAVAGANZA AND DISCO

ENTRY: £2
EVERYONE WELCOME!
...DS TO BE DONATED
...AL FUND

GReeNViLLe ELeMeNTARY

FUNDRAiSeR SPeCiAL

THIS SATURDAY AT 12.00 P.M.
FREE BUFFET, ENTERTAINMENT
EXTRAVAGANZA AND DISCO

ENTRY: £2
EVERYONE WELCOME!
ALL PROCEEDS TO BE DONATED
TO POSTMAN PETE'S LEGAL FUND

GReeNViLLe ELeMeNTARY

FUNDRAiSeR SPeCiAL

THIS SATURDAY AT 12.00 P.M.
FREE BUFFET, ENTERTAINMENT
EXTRAVAGANZA AND DISCO

ENTRY: £2
EVERYONE WELCOME!
ALL PROCEEDS TO BE DONATED
TO POSTMAN PETE'S LEGAL FUND

She and Ms. Mills had put the **POSTERS** all around the town and at the school gates where everyone would see them. What a great idea! I hadn't expected more than a hundred people to turn up, but this way the whole town would find out.

Postman Pete arrived at quarter to twelve. Shortly afterward, the

192

first few guests started lining up at the door. At **TWELVE O'CLOCK SHARP** everything and everyone was in place. I gave Ms. Mills a signal. She blew her whistle to let everyone know that we were open for business.

As people started pouring into the gym, Debra Derby put on a playlist of **CHEERFUL POP MUSIC,** which really added a party atmosphere. I

went to look for Postman Pete, as my next duty was to introduce his speech. As I passed by the entrance, I noticed that there were still hundreds of people lining up to get in. I ran to the kitchen.

## "MRS. MUDGE,

# We Have an Emergency!" I shouted,

pushing open the doors.

Mrs. Mudge looked at me. "What's wrong Mina?"

"How much food did we order? I mean, how many people can we feed?"

"We calculated for about a hundred," she answered.

"That's what I thought. Er ... I'm afraid that **A FEW MORE PEOPLE** have turned up than expected."

Her eyes widened. "A few more? How

many more?"

I frowned. "I'd say about five hundred."

**"FiVe HUNDReD**

**PeOPLe?"** Mrs. Mudge looked

panicked.

"No, no," I said frantically, "I mean

**FiVe HUNDReD MORe**

people … on top of the hundred that we've got food for."

Mrs. Mudge looked like she was about to faint. "We're doomed! Even if I use up the school supplies, I can't prepare food for a five hundred people on my own. Do you have any ideas?"

I thought about it a bit.

"Yes, I do have an idea. Let's start getting the first trays of food out—that should keep everyone going while we prepare more. **Leave the rest to me**. I need to make a phone call."

**197**

I had just enough time to make my call before going back to the gym to introduce Postman Pete.

I scratched around in my pocket for the speech I'd written … only to discover that I'd left my notes in my coat pocket, which was hanging up in a corner of the kitchen. **NeVeR MiND! ON WiTH THe SHOW!**

Debra turned off the music and the room went quiet as everyone turned to **face the stage at the front.**

Good afternoon and welcome to the Greenville Elementary Fundraiser! As you all know, we're here to raise funds for a very special member of our community. I'm sure you'd rather hear from him than listen to me banging on, so without any further ado …

**POSTMAN PETE!!!**

Everybody clapped and cheered.

Postman Pete nodded as I handed him the

microphone and I left the stage, satisfied

that I'd just got away with making the world's shortest speech without anyone noticing.

Thank you, Mina, and thank you all for coming to this special fundraising event. I'm very touched that everyone here at Greenville Elementary and, in fact, in the **WHOLE COMMUNITY** has come together to help me after a very difficult moment in my career. I'm sure that with all of your help, I'll soon be able to repay my debts and afford the one thing that can help me cope with the day-to-day stress of postal duty: **a support cat.** Anyway, hopefully soon I'll be back on my round, and I'll be able to finally deliver all the mail that has been piling up at the **post office for the past month and a half.**

There was the beginning of an applause that ended in muffled mumblings. An old lady next to me muttered, "Did he say we haven't had any mail for six weeks?"

Anyway, it is my great honor to open this **ENTERTAINMENT EXTRAVAGANZA**. I'd like to thank the fine performers who have donated their time and their skill to this event. Please put your hands together for our first act: Bill Crisp and his version of 'Ode to Joy' played on … played on his tuba? How can you play 'Ode to Joy' on just a tuba?

As it turns out, the answer to Postman Pete's question was: not very well. Bill only had a ten-minute set, but it felt like a lifetime. I made a mental note to hire Bill if I were ever in a situation where I needed to **TORTURE** someone.

Next up were the **GREENVILLE GRITLORDS**. They'd decided to play a collection of popular TV theme tunes on the recorder. I looked down at my schedule and nearly died … **TWENTY MINUTES?** They were on for *twenty* minutes? I looked over at Percy in the backstage area trying to tie on his **HOMEMADE ONE-MAN-BAND INSTRUMENT** made out of tins and other rubbish, and held together with rubber bands and string. He was going to perform as Holly's supporting musician. I set an alarm on my phone. I didn't want to miss Holly's performance. Then I headed for the kitchen to see how Helen Mudge was doing.

I **rushed** through the kitchen doors to find that Granny Meera had already arrived and that she and Mrs. Mudge were hard at work **preparing trays of food**.

"Granny Meera!" I said, "Thank you for coming to help!"

She came over and gave me a hug. "Don't worry, Pumpkin, any time!"

"**WiLL there be enough food?**"

"Oh yes, dear, don't worry," she replied, "I've asked my supplier to make an **EMERGENCY DELIVERY** here to the school. I'm sure the food will be a lot healthier than what you had delivered."

I let out a big sigh of relief. "That's great!"

"You don't need to worry about the food, dear, leave it to us," Granny Meera told me. "Helen and I go back a long way. We used to work together."

"And for the first time in years, I'm actually getting to make some **HEALTHY FOOD!**" Mrs. Mudge added.

Granny Meera smiled. "Go on, get out of here, dear. I'm sure you have plenty of things to do, don't worry about us!"

I walked out of the kitchen feeling like a big weight had been lifted. I reached into my back pocket and pulled out a folded piece of paper with the schedule printed on it. As I looked down, something bright caught my eye. I walked toward it, then bent down to pick it up. A neon pink feather. Something told me that Holly had arrived.

I made my way toward the gym. Fortunately, the Greenville Gritlords had just finished.

Suddenly all the lights went out. There was a hissing sound and a sweet smell as the room was filled with smoke from a smoke machine. There was a sound of crashing and scuffling from the stage, then suddenly a spotlight shone directly onto Holly. She was wearing neon pink tights, a pink, feathered dress, black shoes and a pointy black hat. The thing was that, from the front she just looked like a girl in a **RiDiCULOUS PiNK DRESS**, but from the sides and from the back she looked exactly like a **GiANT FLAMiNGO**.

Holly danced around the stage for a bit, **TWiRLiNG AND SKiPPiNG** to the clunking and

plucking sounds of Percy's one-man band. The act was really funny, actually. I was enjoying it, although probably for all the wrong reasons.

Then suddenly Holly **DRAMATiCALLY** paused. She walked toward the front of the stage and grabbed the microphone, looking way out past the back of the hall, straight through all the people watching her and fixing her eyes on the horizon. Then she belted out:

He's the bravest man in town,
see him on his postal round.
Postman Pete has only got one arm
and that is part of his charm.

Postman Pete won't accept defeat!

See him whistle, see him smile,
see him walk for miles and miles.
He's part man and part machine,
delivering letters for the Queen.

Postman Pete, walking down your street!

Postman Pete, so cruelly sued, when it's his butt that was chewed. Who'd have thought his meaty butt would be poisonous to a mutt?

Postman Pete, a dog ate your seat!

The room went quiet and everybody looked over at Postman Pete. His jaw was hanging open. Had Holly gone too far? I mean, it was probably **THE MOST OFFENSIVE SONG**

I had ever heard. But, surprisingly, Postman Pete collected himself and started clapping. Everyone in the room took this as their cue to start **CLAPPING AND CHEERING**.

Holly beamed a satisfied grin as her eyes scanned the room. She was probably looking for Gareth Trumpshaw.

Holly backed away from the stage blowing kisses into the audience and Mr. Norton took the spotlight.

Well, everybody. First of all, we'd like to thank all of our students for their performances ... no matter how **STRANGE**.

A lot of people have worked very hard to make this event happen and the school would like to **thank you aLL**. Now, this event was all about raising money for Postman Pete and ... would you all like to know how much we've raised?

The whole crowd cheered a huge **'YES!!!'**

Mr. Norton turned to his secretary, Miss Austin, who passed him the results in a sealed envelope.

Between the fun run, the party and a few private donations, Greenville Elementary has raised a whopping £4,200 for Postman Pete. Let's have a big round of applause for you all!

The crowd **CLAPPED AND CHEERED**. Postman Pete joined Mr. Norton on stage. As people started taking photos, I noticed Holly creeping closer and closer until she was standing right next to Postman Pete. I should have known that Holly wouldn't miss an opportunity for some good publicity.

Debra Derby started up the disco and everybody began dancing.

**WOW! FOUR THOUSAND TWO HUNDRED POUNDS!**

I wanted to go and look for Holly

to congratulate her, but I had

some **UNFINISHED**

**BUSINESS** ...

As soon as Mr. Norton and Miss Austin

got down from the stage, I cornered them.

"Mr. Norton, Miss Austin! I'm so glad

I've found you! We're having a bit of an

**EMERGENCY IN THE**

**KITCHEN**, could you come with

me straight away?"

They looked at each other and hastily

followed me to the kitchen doors where

**221**

a disgruntled-looking Holly was already waiting.

"Okay Mina, what's the problem?" Mr. Norton asked as we all burst through the kitchen doors, much to Mrs. Mudge and Granny Meera's surprise.

I was about to speak, but Holly butted in.

"You won't believe it, Gareth didn't turn up! I can't believe it! How **DARE** he miss my sweet moves?"

"Holly, I know you're upset," I said patiently, "but we need to talk to Mr. Norton about something important. Mr.

Norton, are you aware that our school meals are really unhealthy? **ALL WE ARE SERVING IS JUNK FOOD**."

Mr. Norton looked very surprised.

"Really? I'm afraid I don't eat lunch at

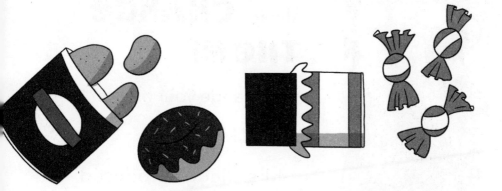

school, but your cook is right here. Let's ask her: Mrs. Mudge, **WHY**

# ARE YOUR MEALS SO UNHEALTHY?"

Mrs. Mudge did not look at all happy.

**"HEY!** I _want_ to prepare healthy meals,

but when I send you

my food orders, you

always **CHANGE**

**THEM!"**

"I change your orders?"

replied Mr. Norton.

Mrs. Mudge produced

a copy of an order she

had emailed Mr. Norton.

**224**

It contained a ton of **HEALTHY INGREDIENTS**. Then she pulled out a delivery note for the same order listing nothing but **UNHEALTHY FOODS**.

Holly interrupted again, "Ugh, and do you know why Gareth Trumpshaw isn't here? It's because he's at the **DENTIST**—he's getting fillings! Can you believe it?"

Mr. Norton looked at the order. "This is very strange. I don't even get these emails. It's my secretary

**MiSS AUSTiN** who puts through the food orders."

Holly was still upset. "He should be watching me, but *oh no*—he's in town visiting **DR. AUSTiN** instead. Can you believe it?"

Suddenly everyone turned to look at Miss Austin, who was slowly backing away toward the door.

I spoke to Holly, "So Holly, are you saying that Gareth is seeing **DR. AUSTiN, THE ONLY DENTiST iN TOWN?**"

"Yes, it's amazing that even someone as **PERFECT** as Gareth has a mouth full of fillings," she sighed dramatically. "Just another side effect of the **AWFUL**

**SCHOOL FOOD** ... and the reason he had to miss my performance."

I looked at Mr. Norton and he looked back at me. I could tell he was thinking exactly the same thing that I was. I turned to speak to **MiSS AUSTiN**.

"Miss Austin, are you and Dr. Austin **ReLATeD?**"

Miss Austin stood in stunned silence. She was looking like a **DeeR CAUGHT iN THe HeADLiGHTS.**

Mr. Norton scratched his head. "You know something ... I do remember you saying that you have a twin sister who is a

dentist, Miss Austin. Mina, I think you may

just have **UNCOVERED A CONSPIRACY**. How did you work it out?"

I didn't want to make a big deal of the whole thing. I didn't want anyone to know that I had arranged a **WHOLE INVESTIGATION**. I'd have to play dumb.

"Oh, it only just occurred to me. I just called you down here because Mrs. Mudge was so upset earlier when the **WRONG FOOD** arrived. But, you know, once Holly mentioned it, it did seem strange that the **ONLY DENTIST AROUND** is also called Austin ..."

At that, Miss Austin broke down.

"Okay, yes ... **I ADMIT iT!** I've been ordering junk food for the school!"

**"BUT WHY?"** said Mrs. Mudge. "It's ruining the children's teeth."

"That's exactly why," I replied. "All the kids in the

school **need to get fillings**, and they have to go to Dr. Austin. Dr. Austin gives her sister a **SHARE OF THE MONEY** for every patient that she sends her."

Miss Austin didn't say anything, she just nodded.

Mr. Norton stepped forward. "Well, it may have been an accident, Mina, but the school owes you our gratitude.

You've helped save a lot of people from **DENTAL DiSASTERS**.

Now, Miss Austin, you'd better come with me. I think we need to talk."

# LOG ENTRY #7

Location: At home, in bedroom
Status: Finishing up my notes

It's been a week since the charity fun run

and since we uncovered the truth about the

**Loathsome school Lunches**.

Miss Austin is no longer working at

the school, and as for her sister, she

has left town. I walked past the dental

234

surgery yesterday, it looks like it's been **CLOSeD DOWN**.

**School Lunches** are healthy again and Mrs. Mudge is enjoying her job preparing **FRESH AND DELICIOUS FOOD**. I've found a dentist in a neighboring town and I have an appointment to get two fillings later. Hopefully they will be the last for a while …

**OH!** And on last Monday's issue of the Greenville Gazette, you can read the headline: '**GREENVILLE ELEMENTARY RAISES SMALL FORTUNE FOR CHARITY!**' Underneath, there's a

# Greenville Gazette

## GREENVILLE ELEMENTARY RAISES SMALL FORTUNE FOR LOCAL MAN!

huge photo of Mr. Norton handing Postman Pete a check, next to what looks like a giant flamingo! I'd say that Holly had succeeded in getting publicity, but I'm not sure that anyone will recognize her …

So I guess life is back to **NORMAL** now. I got home from school half an hour ago and finished writing up this case. Later, I might write something **BORiNG** in my **DeCOY DiARY**, but now I'm going into the back of my wardrobe to put this file away.

# THE CASE OF
# THE LOATHSOME
# SCHOOL LUNCHES:

# LOOK OUT FOR THE NEXT MINA MISTRY INVESTIGATION

# MINA MISTRY (SORT OF) INVESTIGATES THE CASE OF THE DISAPPEARING PETS